A Rhinoceros Wakes Me Up in the Morning

A Bedtime Tale by Peter Goodspeed

Pictures by Dennis Panek

Puffin Books

Penguin Books Ltd, Harmondsworth, Middlesex, England
Penguin Books, 40 West 23rd Street, New York, New York 10010, U.S.A.
Penguin Books Australia Ltd, Ringwood, Victoria, Australia
Penguin Books Canada Limited, 2801 John Street, Markham, Ontario, Canada L3R 1B4
Penguin Books (N.Z.) Ltd, 182–190 Wairau Road, Auckland 10, New Zealand

First published by Bradbury Press, 1982
Published in Picture Puffins 1984
Reprinted 1984
Library of Congress Cataloging in Publication Data
Goodspeed, Peter.   A rhinoceros wakes me up in the morning.
Summary: A zoo of stuffed animals helps a small boy through his daily activities.
[1. Stories in rhyme.   2. Toys—Fiction]   I. Panek, Dennis, ill.   II. Title.
PZ8.3.G629Rh   1984   [E]   83-19175   ISBN 0-14-050455-9

Printed in the United States of America
by General Offset Company, Inc., Jersey City, New Jersey

For Antonia
— P.G.

A rhinoceros wakes me up in the morning,

An elephant brushes my teeth;

A porcupine follows me down the stairs,

A panther hides underneath.

A dragon burns toast in the kitchen,

A beaver grinds oats for my gruel;

A gibbon stuffs lunch in my book bag,

A unicorn takes me to school.

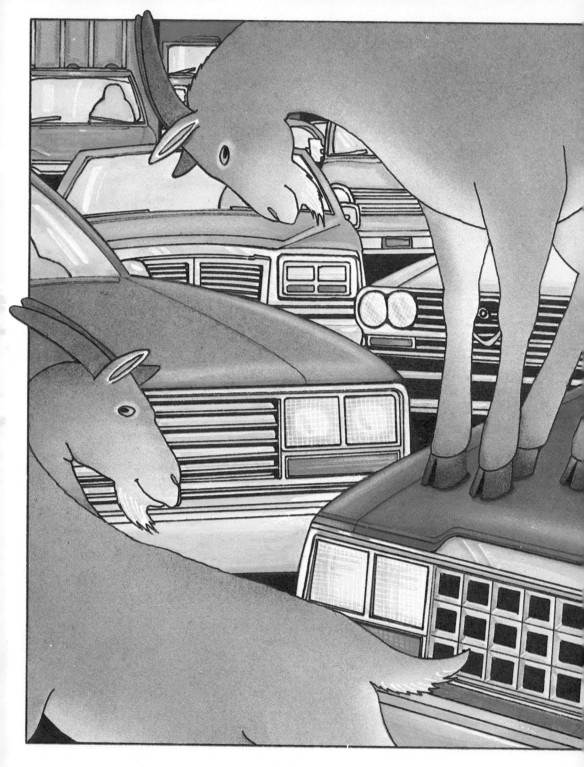

Two billy goats tie up the traffic,

A crocodile cries the whole way;

A giraffe watches over the school yard,

A parrot shouts rules as we play.

A dinosaur takes names of who's talking,

A dormouse winds up the clock;

A peacock gives brushes for painting,

A packrat makes off with the chalk.

A camel drops me near home again,

A grizzly bear waits at the gate;

A rabbit whips up a rare cheese sauce,

A penguin skates on my plate.

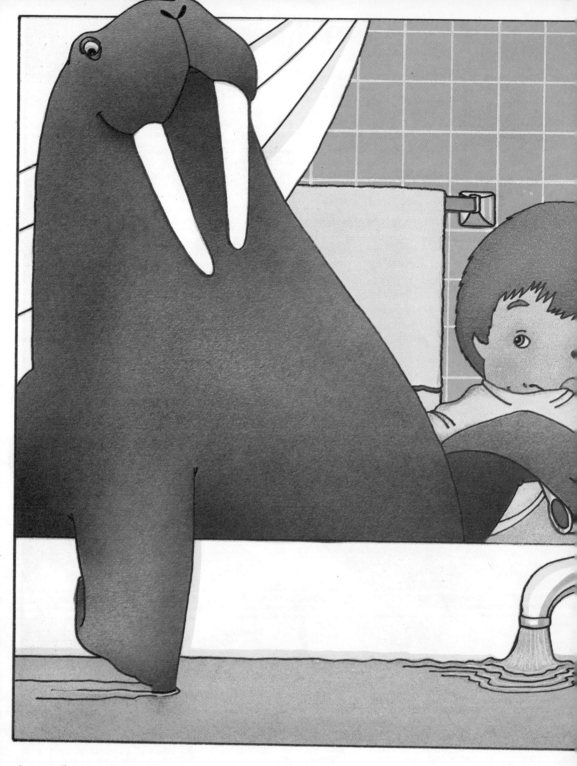

A walrus draws water for bathing,

A raccoon gets lost in shampoo;

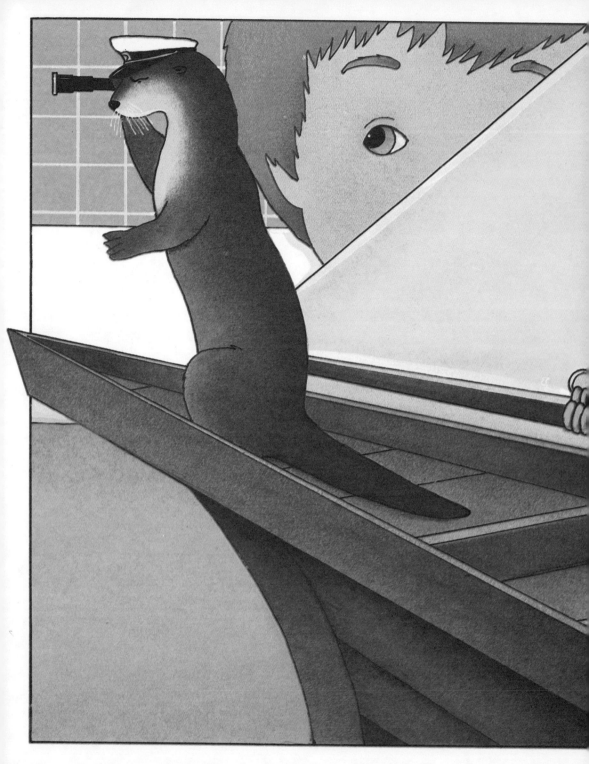

An otter sets sail in my ocean,

A hippopotamus serves as the crew.

A zebra gets my pajamas,

A panda tucks me in tight;

A toad stands guard in the doorway,

My zoo settles down for the night.

DISCARDED